Oxford University Press, Great Clarendon Street, Oxford OX2 6DP

Oxford   New York
Athens   Auckland   Bangkok   Bogota   Bombay
Buenos Aires   Calcutta   Cape Town   Dar es Salaam   Delhi
Florence   Hong Kong   Istanbul   Karachi
Kuala Lumpur   Madras   Madrid   Melbourne
Mexico City   Nairobi   Paris   Singapore
Taipei   Tokyo   Toronto   Warsaw
and associated companies in
Berlin Ibadan

Oxford is a trade mark of Oxford University Press

Text © Sheila Lavelle 1994
Illustrations © Susan Scott 1994

First published 1994
First published in paperback 1996
Reprinted in paperback
with new cover 1997

ISBN 0 19 272271 9

A CIP catalogue record for this book is available
from the British Library

Printed in Hong Kong

Snowy
The Christmas Dog

Written by Sheila Lavelle
Illustrated by Susan Scott

Oxford University Press

It was Emma who heard the dog on the roof on Christmas morning, after dreaming of sleighbells jingling and reindeer's hoofbeats in the snow.

She woke up in her room in the attic, and at first she couldn't believe her ears.

She sat up and listened. Then she heard it again and this time she knew she was right.

Emma jumped out of bed and ran along the landing to her sister's room.

'Katie, wake up,' she said, shaking her shoulder. 'There's a dog on the roof.'

Katie groaned and pulled her pillow over her head.

'Don't be stupid, Emma,' she said. 'How could there be?'

There was more barking and yelping from just above their heads, and Emma dashed back to her room.

She stood on the bed and unfastened the catch on the skylight window, banging upwards on the frame.

A blast of air made her hair stand on end as the window flew open and let in the cold December morning.

Emma stuck her head outside. Snow was falling fast, and a thick covering lay on the roof and on the roofs of the houses all around.

Then Emma noticed something very strange.

Here and there on the roof, quickly disappearing under fresh flakes, were footprints in the snow.

Emma stared, remembering her dream.

The footprints looked as if they had been made by a large pair of wellies, and there were others that could have been the prints of hooves.

There were even some grooves that looked like marks from the runners of a sleigh.

Don't be stupid, Emma, said Emma to herself, and blinked the snow out of her eyes.

The barking began again, and it was then that Emma saw a small white shape beside the chimney pot.

'Katie, it *is* a dog,' she called. 'Come and see.'

The dog pricked up his ears at the sound of Emma's voice. He stared at her hopefully, then threw back his head and howled at the sky.

'Good grief,' said Katie, appearing in Emma's doorway. 'How did it get up there?'

She pushed Emma out of the way and put her head out of the window.

'Go and get Mum and Gran,' she said. 'We'll have to get him down.'

It was the strangest Christmas morning Emma had ever had.

There was the excitement of Mum climbing out on
the roof in her dressing-gown and almost falling off.

There was the thrill of getting the dog down at last
by tempting him with a cold sausage.

There were all the arguments about how the dog had
got there and who he belonged to and what they were
going to do with him.

Emma even forgot to open her presents.

Emma and Katie rubbed the dog with a towel and gave him some milk.

'Go and look in the front room,' said Gran. 'You haven't seen what Father Christmas has brought you.'

Katie laughed. 'There's no such person as Father Christmas,' she said scornfully.

But she ran with Emma to unwrap the pile of parcels under the Christmas tree all the same.

After breakfast Mum phoned the police.

'Nobody has reported a dog missing,' she said, when she came back into the kitchen. 'I said we'd keep him here until he's claimed. He seems a nice little dog now that he's dry. What shall we call him?'

Emma looked at the dog's fluffy coat. 'Let's call him Snowy,' she said, 'because we found him in the snow.'

What nobody could agree about was how the dog came to be on the roof in the first place. Katie said he must have fallen out of an aeroplane, Gran thought he must have come down by parachute, and Mum thought he must have been put there by somebody having a joke. Emma didn't think it was a very funny joke.

All day she kept thinking of her dream, and of the sleighbells, and of those strange footprints in the snow.

Nobody came forward to claim him, and Snowy became Emma's dog. He followed her everywhere, and he slept on her bed in the attic.

Emma took him for walks every day after school. She fed him and brushed him, and she saved up her pocket-money to buy him a collar and lead.

When summer came, Emma took Snowy for picnics by the river.

He even went with the family for a holiday by the sea. Snowy didn't seem to like hot weather much, and spent most of his time looking for somewhere cool to lie down.

'He is a funny dog,' said Gran one day. 'He keeps trying to curl up in the fridge!'

'He likes cold places,' said Emma. 'Perhaps he comes from the North Pole.'

'Don't be stupid, Emma,' said Gran. 'There aren't any dogs at the North Pole. Only polar bears.'

Emma said nothing more, but she gave Snowy an
ice-cube to lick whenever she got the chance.

Snowy had everything a dog could wish for, but he never completely settled down.

Emma would watch him sometimes as he lay in the garden with his nose on his paws, gazing up at the sky.

She knew that he would never be happy in his new home. He seemed to be waiting for something, or for somebody.

Emma would look at his sad brown eyes and wish that she could help.

Autumn came, and then winter.

Snowy became more and more restless as Christmas came round once again.

He spent more and more time in the attic, sitting on Emma's bed, watching the sky through the skylight window.

On Christmas Eve it began to snow.

'Whatever's the matter with that dog?' said Mum, shooing him off the bed for the hundredth time. 'He keeps gazing into the sky. I can't imagine why.'

'He wants to get out on the roof,' said Emma.

'Don't be stupid, Emma,' said Mum. 'What would he want to do that for?'

When Emma went to bed she lay in the dark for a long time, stroking the dog's ears and thinking.

If she was right about Snowy, there was only one thing to do. And tonight was the only night she could do it.

Emma thought and thought, and at last she made up her mind.

It was Snowy's whining that woke her a few hours later, from a dream of sleighbells jingling and reindeer's hoofbeats in the snow.

Emma sat up and listened.

She hadn't been dreaming.

Real sleighbells were jingling, real hooves were clip-clopping, and somebody in big wellies was stamping about on the roof above Emma's head.

Snowy went wild. He jumped up at the skylight, barking and wagging his tail.

Emma knew she had no time to waste. She stood up on the bed and flung the window open, letting in a gust of cold wind and a flurry of snow.

She hugged Snowy tightly to her for a moment.

'Goodbye, Snowy,' she said into his fur, and bundled him out on to the roof. With a quick lick at her face the dog was gone.

Emma heard Snowy barking, and then she heard something else that made her shiver with excitement in her pyjamas.

'So that's where you are!' said a deep voice that made Emma think of plum pudding and mince pies. 'Did you fall off the sleigh last Christmas Eve? We'd better make sure that doesn't happen again, hadn't we?'

Hooves drummed on the roof, there was a sudden jingling of bells, and then silence.

Emma closed the window and went back to bed.

She knew she would miss him, but only one thing really mattered.

Snowy was on his way home.